Parsley Sage, Rosemary & Time

Parsley Sage,
Rosemary &
Time

JANE LOUISE CURRY

Illustrated by Charles Robinson

A MARGARET K. MCELDERRY BOOK

Atheneum 1975

New York

*For James,
the magician's son.*

Library of Congress Cataloging in Publication Data

Curry, Jane Louise.
Parsley Sage, Rosemary, and time.
"A Margaret K. McElderry book."
SUMMARY: Ten-year-old Rosemary thinks the word
"Time" cut into a stone in her aunt's old herb garden
should be spelled "Thyme" until she picks a sprig of
the herb around it and discovers herself back in the
eighteenth century.
[1. Space and time—Fiction. 2. Witchcraft—Fiction]
I. Robinson, Charles, 1931-   ill. II. Title. PZ7.C936
     Par   [Fic]   74-18181   ISBN 0-689-50019-x

Published simultaneously in Canada by
McClelland & Stewart, Ltd.
Manufactured in the United States of America
Printed by The Murray Printing Compny
Forge Village, Massachusetts
Bound by H. Wolff, New York
First Edition

Contents

Aunt Sibby

Rosemary was to go to Aunt Sibby.

To Rosemary, a solemn child, that was alarming news. Mother called Aunt Sibby "a most distressing young woman," and more than once Rosemary had seen Father raise his eyebrows and exclaim, "Why, the little witch!" while reading a letter from his sister. Aunt Sibby had never come to Washington, so Rosemary did not remember her, though they had met in the Salem Hospital when Rosemary was born, and again at Granny Walpole's when she was two. Aunt Sibby had since then been living in France and Wales. And San Francisco. And New Mexico.

Aunt Sibby made, it was said, pots of money from writing detective stories, but not even money had made Aunt Sibby respectable. Once she had gone shopping with Mother at Lord and Taylor in Boston in her stocking feet, and Mother had to pretend she didn't know her. Blisters from a forty-mile hike down the Appalachian Trail from Mount Katahdin were no excuse. And both Mother and Father shuddered when they told of arriving at the Colony House Motor Lodge on the first night of their honeymoon—without a stick of luggage. The trunk of the car was full of rabbits. Aunt Sibby's handiwork.

Nevertheless, since the State Department's Commercial Section had ordered Father off to China on a fact-finding tour of tractor factories, Rosemary was being packed off to visit Aunt Sibby. The trip had come up suddenly when Father's superior, who was to have made the tour, came down with the Asiatic flu. Most unfortunately, Granny Walpole, to whom Rosemary usually went when her parents were off fact-finding, was in the hospital with a broken hip. Since Mother was a Total Orphan, with no family at all, the choice came down to Aunt Sibby or Camp Winniwippi. But the fees for ten weeks at Camp Winniwippi would, Mother thought, be more wisely spent on Chinese antiques. Granny, telephoning from her hospital bed, supposed that Sibby *was* the last resort. "But don't give her a chance to argue, for she will," was Granny's advice. "She'll be at home all summer and may as well prove useful."

Mother took the hint, and Aunt Sibby duly received a reply-paid telegram reading: MEET ROSEMARY AMERICAN AIRLINES FLIGHT 300 BOSTON TWENTIETH JUNE STOP URGENT MISSION CHINA STOP THANKS REGARDS AFFECTIONATELY MARIAN AND QUINCY.

That was on the nineteenth, which gave Aunt Sibby *very* little chance to argue. Her reply was unsigned but characteristic: QUERY COLON WHAT WOULD YOU HAVE DONE IF I HAD SAID NO.

At Boston's Logan Airport, Aunt Sibby turned out to be the pretty, black-haired, green-eyed young woman in the cream silk pant suit. Catching sight of Rosemary in the stream of passengers, she stopped in mid-stride and stared—not a "How tall you've grown!" stare, but a Perplexed and Startled one.

"Rosemary? Rosemary Walpole?" Aunt Sibby tilted her head quizzically, as if Rosemary were a jigsaw-puzzle piece that didn't fit. Then she grinned.

"Red hair! Aren't you lucky! You're not like your father at all. I was half-expecting a cod-faced little priss."

Rosemary's eyes widened. *Cod*-faced? Her father? Father was *handsome*. And quite perfect, according to Mother. If Rosemary had wondered once or twice whether he wasn't a shade more pleased with himself than he ought to be, it was quite understandable. "If you're the best at what you do, why pretend you're not?" Mother always said.

"H-how do you do, Aunt Sibby?" Rosemary stammered, remembering her manners.

Aunt Sibby laughed and enveloped her in a hard, sweet-smelling hug. "Good heavens, a sobersides at ten! Now. Come along to the baggage area. While we wait for your luggage, I can ask embarrassing questions, and you can practice being shocked, like your mother." Aunt Sibby's left eye drooped in a hint of a wink.

Rosemary, feeling an unfamiliar excitement, hurried after her. Aunt Sibby was *horrid*.

Aunt Sibby's car was long and low and also cream-colored. Rosemary's smaller case took up most of her foot room. The larger had to be wedged upright in the space behind the seats. *Not a practical car*, Mother would have said.

"Tell me," said Aunt Sibby, as she helped Rosemary with her safety-belt buckle, "did your father try to disconnect the safety-belt buzzers under the front seat of that new Mercedes he bought?"

Rosemary nodded.

"Ha!" Aunt Sibby sounded immensely satisfied.

"I always told him he would grow up to be an idiot, and he never disappoints me." She fastened her own belt and turned the ignition key. "Now, I'll drive, and *you* can ask embarrassing questions."

Rosemary couldn't think of a one, and as the car whipped forward she forgot about everything but holding her hair down so that it wouldn't whip in the wind. She had never before ridden in a sports car. The speed was quite alarming once they were on the parkway. At least it *felt* so—but the speedometer (which Rosemary watched warily out of the corner of her eye) hovered reassuringly close to the speed limit. It was having the top down that did it. Aunt Sibby's long, black hair flickered in the wind they made.

All too soon they were in Salem, pulling up in front of Granny Walpole's house. After a quick sandwich and a visit to Granny in the hospital, they set out for Bennickport, in Maine, where Aunt Sibby had bought a house—the same house the Walpoles had rented every summer when Sibby and her brother, Rosemary's father, were children.

"I always loved it," Aunt Sibby explained, as they soared past Portsmouth, New Hampshire, and over the bridge into Maine. "So, when the old owner died this spring, I conjured up enough money and bought it."

She looked so impressively witchy when she

said "conjured"—her long, black locks flying every which-a-way and her green eyes sparkling—that Rosemary giggled.

When they reached the far side of Bennickport, she wished she hadn't.

The weatherbeaten sign on Aunt Sibby's tall, stone gatepost said:

WYCHWOOD

Rosemary folded her hands primly in her lap as the car dipped down the gravel drive. *Wychwood.* What could it mean? "Which Wood"? That made little sense. Walpoles (except for Aunt Sibby) were sensible people, as Mother always said with an approving nod from Father. But it couldn't mean "Witch" Wood either. It was impossible to imagine Father or Granny Walpole living in a house that called itself Witch Wood.

Or one so overgrown with rose vines and ankle-deep in grass.

The house might, in fact, have passed for the world's largest rosebush if here and there a pane of glass had not gleamed and a few dark shingles showed beneath the rose leaves. Two chimneys and a row of gables stuck timid snouts out along the roof line.

Rosemary eyed the grass with disapproval. "Don't you have a lawnmower?"

"Was that an embarrassing question?" Aunt

Sibby, unloading the suitcases, laughed. "I have one, but it feels nicer in bare feet this way."

"I'm not allowed to go in bare feet," said Rosemary virtuously. "Mother says I might catch Attley's Foot or chiggers."

"Not here," said Aunt Sibby. Her solemn look twitched a little at the corners. "No Attleys ever lived here, and I don't think chiggers come this far north. But you can please yourself." She nodded at the front door and it opened. Just like that. Nod. Open.

Rosemary, following nervously with the smaller case, was quite relieved to see a stout little woman in a flowered bib apron behind the door. It had not, after all, opened itself. Rosemary felt silly for having thought it might.

"Rosemary, this is Mrs. Helps."

"I see you made it in one piece again," Mrs. Helps said tartly to Aunt Sibby. "Phone's been ringing all day, so supper'll be late. I might's well be a social secretary." She eyed Rosemary critically. "Cat's got your tongue, I see. Well, you just come along to the kitchen while your auntie reads her phone messages. There's lemonade, and I'd best comb the snarls out of your hair. That dreadful car's blown it into a nasty orange dust mop."

In the kitchen Mrs. Helps turned and caught a glimmer suspiciously like a tear. "There, there, dear, I *am* sorry!" she exclaimed. "Don't you mind

a crotchety old woman. I never meant orange. It's
not orange at all, but the nicest red I've seen since
George Potts went off."

It would not be polite, Rosemary decided, to ask
what George Potts went off to.

Mrs. Helps reached down a fat cookie jar,
poured a glass of lemonade, and sat Rosemary
down at the kitchen table before bustling off in
search of a comb. "And you mustn't mind about
your auntie any more'n me. I've known her ever
since she was a little thing. She's not *all* nonsense."

"In fact,"—the words floated down the back
stairs—"she'll soon have you bewitched like everybody else."

Parsley Sage

For a sensible child, Rosemary found herself with a head full of the most nonsensical questions. Obviously Aunt Sibby and Wychwood (did it *really* mean only Elm Wood?) were . . . unusual. But were they interesting-unusual or downright-peculiar-unusual?

Rosemary was confident that there was no such thing as magic. Her mother had long ago explained that the words "magic" and "mystery" were used only by people with minds too lazy to find the facts and organize them into explanations. Mother was extremely good at organizing facts. Father called her his "treasure" and, when he was in a particularly jovial mood, his "Handy-Dandy-Little-Fact-Finder."

But what was one to do with such peculiar facts? One was an ancient tortoiseshell cat with arthritis, who creaked around the house—but when Aunt Sibby flickered her fingers and crooned *Miminy, miminy, tall as a chi-mi-ny*, danced on his hind legs like a kitten. He was so old that (except when Aunt Sibby called *Fitchy, fitchy, libberty gizzard!*) it took him five minutes to creak from the sun porch door to his bowl by the kitchen fireplace.

His name was Parsley Sage. His last name was Sage, rather than Walpole, because, as Aunt Sibby said in the drawling voice she used when she was having a private joke, "He's no more Walpole-ish than I am." He was twenty years old.

And what sort of fact was Aunt Sibby's missing supper that evening, and Mrs. Helps' grumbled explanation that she'd flown off in a lotus to London for dinner? Or her return at the last clock-chime of midnight—even though London was on the opposite side of the Atlantic Ocean?

Then, too, there was Mr. Helps. Mr. Helps brought Mrs. Helps along after breakfast and stayed to prune back the rose vines "so's them shingles don't get the damp rot." Mr. Helps was smaller even than Mrs. Helps. He had a tall squiff of sandy hair like a Munchkin and winked at Rosemary every time he saw her as if to say, "*We* know." Know *what*?

Rosemary sat on the sun porch steps, chin in hand, frowning over it all. While she sat there, Parsley Sage appeared, creaking along the flagstone path from the front of the house, his tail flicking like a lazy metronome. As he passed, he slid a secret sideways look at a startled Rosemary and—could cats smile?—smiled.

Parsley's tail flicked again. Flicker-flick. "Come," it seemed to beckon. "Come see."

Not until the cat had disappeared through a tangle of roses growing midway along the tall back hedge did Rosemary follow. There, under the rose creepers, she spied an arched wooden trellis and, like a curtain on the far side, another thorny thatch of roses.

Rosemary parted the vines to edge her way through, but the moment she let go of one to push back another, the first caught fast in her hair or T-shirt. She backed out gingerly, snagged and tousled.

Clearly, the only way through was Parsley's way. Rosemary dropped to her stomach and wriggled her way underneath, emerging, red-faced and scratched, into a second garden, wild and lovely, and as quiet as a woods-creature hiding from a hunter.

It was quite large. A tall stone wall bounded three sides. The fourth was the high hedge with its rose-arbor barrier. Within, birches grew in lacy clusters along the wall, and willows. Across the wall, on the woods side, tall trees leaned and whispered in the green shade. The two closest up against the wall were giant elms, the like of which Rosemary had never seen. Their limbs were as thick as full-grown tree trunks, arching up and out to shield the garden from the morning sun. Rhododendrons and azaleas bloomed like candelabra in the shadows, and the knee-high grass was powdered with wildflowers.

Parsley was nowhere to be seen, but his trail led like a ribbon through the feathery grass. Rosemary found him waiting at the far end of the garden, sitting on a stepping stone beside a straggly bush.

"Nice cat," said Rosemary. Never having had a cat (or, for that matter, a dog or bird or mouse), she was not sure what sort of conversation they preferred. Old Parsley watched her so expectantly that she felt she ought to say *some*thing. "Pretty kitty?"

Parsley got up, stretched, and—quite pointedly—looked down at the round, flat stone where he stood. Rosemary's first thought was that he had been offended at the "kitty," but that of course was silly. Then she saw, beside his paw, a green *P* and after it other letters: letters cut in the stone long ago and now filled up with moss. As she bent closer to see what it said, Parsley thoughtfully moved around to the stone on the other side of the scrubby bush, and then to a third.

The first two moss-lettered stones read PARSLEY and SAGE.

"Oh!" gasped Rosemary. And then, with a nervous giggle: "How funny."

Parsley twitched a disdainful ear and moved on. Rosemary, alarmed but determined, followed.

Parsley's third stone read ROSEMARY.

The mossy letters of the fourth spelled out TIME.

The cat stepped back to PARSLEY and began calmly to groom himself.

PARSLEY SAGE. ROSEMARY. And TIME.

Parsley, Sage, Rosemary, and Time. But in an herb garden, oughtn't it to be spelled *t-h-y-m-e?* For it was, of course, simply an herb garden. Other stones, some so overgrown with moss that they looked like fat, green cushions, marked once-upon-a-time patches of catnip, lavender, camomile, basil, and chives. While the rosemary and sage had grown lank and woody and the chives had thrived, spreading out into the grass, the others—all but one—had died away.

The exception was the flourishing green mat around the TIME stone. It grew thickly, about six inches high, and its leaves were darkly, glossily green and shaped like tiny crows' feet. Rosemary pinched off a sprig and sniffed it.

It smelled like . . . Rosemary wasn't sure *what* it smelled like. At first it was Granny Walpole's musty attic and dusty boxes of old clothes and keepsakes. The second sniff was quite different, sharp and sweet together, and as fresh as a breeze in a pine wood.

Parsley looked for all the world frozen in mid-yawn. He sat with his back to the garden wall and grinned and grinned and grinned.

"Stop that," said Rosemary irritably. "It looks silly." When Parsley did not move, she looked behind her, but nothing moved there either.

Nothing. Nothing at all. The tangled garden was utterly, eerily still.

Not a leaf rustled. Not a fly buzzed. A downy woodpecker on a birch branch perched open-mouthed, staring, as still as Parsley—who hadn't twitched a whisker. A column of ants, snaking across the ROSEMARY stone, stood at a dead halt.

Rosemary shivered. "I don't think I like this garden after all," she announced loudly. "It's too messy."

Parsley grinned on.

"You stop that, cat!" snapped Rosemary, her voice rising. "Or I'll come step on your tail."

Parsley only grinned and stared.

And then Rosemary saw what he and the woodpecker stared at.

The woodpecker's mate.

The woodpecker's mate, swooping over the wall from the elm wood, had stopped in midair.

And hung there.

A Patch of Time

Everything but Rosemary was stopped. Everything in sight. Stopped still. Stopped in the middle of . . . whatever. Flies hung in mid-flight. A measuring worm paused in mid-reach.

Rosemary's hands flew to her mouth in astonishment. The sprig of thyme she was holding dropped to the ground.

At just that moment, as unaccountably as it had stopped, everything started up again. Old Parsley skirted the patch of thyme in a low crouch. The female woodpecker flicked down past his too-slow paw and up into the birch tree. All the summer sounds came whispering back. Parsley, the bird forgotten, watched Rosemary expectantly.

Rosemary drew an uncertain breath. She hadn't seen what she saw. Couldn't have. She'd had a "touch of the sun," as Mother put it. "Always, *always* wear a hat out of doors in the heat of day, dear. Too much sun will make you giddy."

And she did feel giddy. The floppy straw hat that lay squashed flat at the bottom of her suitcase: that was what she needed. "Besides, it's nearly lunchtime," she added aloud. Retrieving the sprig of thyme, she stuffed it into her jeans' pocket and hurried to the rose arbor.

Once past the curtain of roses, Rosemary dawdled toward the sun porch, thorn-snaggled and uneasy. The sun wasn't, after all, all *that* hot.

Mr. Helps and his clippers were up a ladder, hard at work on the roses hiding the eaves. The lawn was littered with cuttings.

"*There* you are," Mr. Helps called cheerily. "The missus was just asking after you. Poked your way back into that jungle, eh? One of these days I mean to—"

He stopped abruptly, mouth open, clippers aloft, one foot on the ladder and one in the air. A handful of rose cuttings tossed to the pile below hung motionless halfway there. Parsley Sage, trotting across the grass, stood poised on a single paw, unmoving.

Rosemary herself froze. It had happened again. It had happened the moment her fingers closed around the sprig of thyme. Sprig of *Time*. Time . . .

Rosemary's heart went skittery-thump.

Carefully, she withdrew her hand from her pocket, empty.

In the same moment Parsley took another step and Mr. Helps said, ". . . get around to clearing out—" Then both Parsley and Mr. Helps stopped just as abruptly as they had started, for Rosemary had thrust her hand back into her pocket to clutch the leafy twig and ran like sixty.

Upstairs, Rosemary half-filled a glass at the bathroom sink and popped the twig into it. Outside the open bathroom window she heard Mr. Helps on his ladder finish his dangling sentence with ". . . some of that tangle." He paused.

"Now where in tarnation'd that child disappear to?" he muttered. "Right there, glum as an onion she was. Then, *phhht!* Gone, quick as a wink."

Rosemary stared at the twig in the glass.

Every time she touched the thyme, time stopped. Except for her.

Mrs. Helps rang an old brass handbell to call everyone to lunch. Aunt Sibby had been planting primroses out front and came into the pantry to wash her grimy hands. She found a brushed and tidied Rosemary studying a bottle in the spice rack.

"What's that? Thyme?" asked Aunt Sibby. "Do you like to cook? Or are you a secret herb-muncher?"

"Actually neither," said Rosemary seriously. "Except I do like to chew mint. We grow it in our flower garden at home." She hesitated. "Is this always spelled this way?"

" 'Thyme'? I think so. Why?"

Rosemary shook the bottle thoughtfully. "What does it look like when it's not all dry and crinkled?"

The question went unanswered, for a scowling Mrs. Helps appeared in the kitchen doorway. "Won't be *my* fault if your cold soup's warm and your sandwiches dried out." She sniffed. "If you don't want to eat, we can save the soup for when that gentleman comes to dinner tonight."

Rosemary and her aunt obediently went in to lunch. For a simple meal of soup and sandwiches, it took forever to get through. The leaves that nestled in Rosemary's pocket, pinched from the sprig of thyme, became a terrible temptation, but she resisted it. She had the uneasy feeling that Aunt Sibby would know if time stopped and Rosemary slipped away. . . .

After lunch, in the library-sitting-room, Aunt Sibby searched the shelves of old books that had come with the house and the boxes of books not yet unpacked from her moving three months earlier. "You've reminded me that I *have* got something that tells about thyme." What she turned up was an old leatherbound volume with gold lettering on its spine that read *A Moderne Herball.*

Each herb in the book was pictured in a delicate woodcut and described according to its "virtues," which meant, Aunt Sibby explained, its healing powers.

"Boil the leaves of Rosemary in white wine," the *Herball* advised, "and thou shalt have a fair Face. Parsley "comforteth the Stomick and the Hart," it said, and "Why should a Man die whose Garden groweth Sage?" As for thyme, it was not only spelled with both the *h* and *y*, but the picture of the herb looked nothing at all like Rosemary's "time."

Aunt Sibby frowned. "I had an idea that this book spelled it *t-i-m-e,* but apparently not. I wonder where . . ."

"It doesn't really matter," said Rosemary hastily. It wouldn't do to have her aunt remembering the stones in the old herb garden where she must have played as a child—not, at least, until Rosemary had discovered for herself what it all meant. "I guess it was a silly question."

Aunt Sibby sighed.

Aunt Sibby's interest in Rosemary had fallen off considerably, to tell the truth, though she had been entertained by the question at breakfast about flying lotuses. The cream-colored car was, it transpired, a Lotus; and the London dinner had been in London, New Hampshire. Perhaps the turning point had been Rosemary's cutting her luncheon sandwich precisely into fours and refusing to answer a question until she had chewed the one bite twenty times. For some reason that had seemed to depress Aunt Sibby.

She continued, of course, to be perfectly kind. She pointed out interesting books about long-ago Bennickport settlers and the Abenaki Indians for whom Bennick and Bennickport had been named. She suggested tomorrow's matinee of *The Ivory Door* at the Playhouse, after a picnic lunch on the beach. But these were dutiful kindnesses, offered with a faint quirk of an ironical eyebrow.

Rosemary politely leafed through the pages of engravings of neat cabins and trim houses, quaintly dressed colonists, and dignified Indians with closed faces. She tried not to look superior when told that *The Ivory Door* was a fairy-tale play by the author of *Pooh*. But at the picnic proposal she shivered.

"On the sand? But food always gets so *gritty*."

"Well, then," said Aunt Sibby drily, "we'll go to Cape Tortoise and eat lobster rolls on the dock for lunch tomorrow."

At any other time, her aunt's thinly disguised disappointment would have set Rosemary to puzzling out the why of it, and Trying Harder. Now all she could think of was slipping away to the tangled back garden and the patch of time.

The Sundial

The time patch was a fact. And facts, as Rosemary's parents so often repeated, are connected to other facts and add up to explanations. That was what Rosemary meant to discover: a sensible explanation.

Parsley went along, keeping so close underfoot that twice Rosemary trod on his tail. Each time, after an offended screech, there he was, underfoot again.

"Afraid you'll miss something? Go on, or shoo!" Rosemary stopped at the briar-rose barrier. With a pair of kitchen shears filched for the purpose, she set about enlarging the thorny passage into the back garden. She cut away trailing ends and snipped away as many thorn-tips as she could reach, gaining the wild garden as quickly and considerably more tidily than before.

The garden was quiet but sunny now, and less mysterious. A small stone slab earlier hidden in shadow leaned against a sunny ivied wall. On it was engraved HERE LYES TOPHET MY DEARE CATT. Nearby—Rosemary had not noticed it before—an odd metal bracket stuck straight out from among the ivy leaves.

Stepping from the CATNIP stone to LAVENDER to TIME, Rosemary reached out to touch the bracket's tip. It could not be for hanging flower-pots on, for it curved downward slightly at the end. Odd. On impulse she pulled at the ivy, parting the leaves that covered the thick tangle of vines. Underneath, the gleam of metal caught her eye: metal, and on it rayed lines and what might be the Roman numeral III.

"M-mrow-l," said Parsley. He pushed between her feet and rubbed his whiskers on the knot of Rosemary's shoelaces, a friendly gesture that almost got him stepped on again, for she hardly noticed him.

Rosemary was too intent on the ivy. One yank freed a thick vine that, jerked again, loosened a whole patch of leaf and vine. With a bit of pulling and puffing, the whole swatch came away, revealing most of a large, metal circle set in the wall. The air sparkled with dust, and long-dead leaves rattled down to rest in the trampled grass and the time patch. Parsley and Rosemary both sneezed.

It was a sundial. A sundial as old as the weathered wall. There was the sun's face with a halo of rays. The curious metal bracket was set to catch the shadow from the real sun and at the same time serve the face as a long Pinocchio-nose. A very odd and watchful face.

"How very un*u*sual!" observed Rosemary, in just the satisfied tone her mother used in remarking upon interesting antique whatnots. "I'll bet nobody's seen it for—for a hundred years."

Then, recollecting why she had returned to the garden, she pulled a folded piece of paper and a stubby pencil from her jeans' pocket and sat herself down on the TIME stone. *Time Facts*, she wrote at the top. Below came *Sientiffic Investigation*, and below that, *Sensery Evidense*. Rosemary was a very erratic speller.

After *Sensery Evidense* came a list of the five senses. "Touch" and "Smell" she had already investigated. After a moment's thought she squeezed in "Eating" after "Taste." Then, getting down on her knees beside the green mat of time, she licked at the tip of a twig, where feathery new leaves grew. The taste of it sparkled on the tongue like mint, yet wasn't at all minty.

Rosemary chewed at the pencil for a long moment. Finally, after "Taste," she wrote (very unscientifically), "Like Christmas morning." It was

the closest she could come to the excited wakeful-
ness she felt. *Every*thing sparkled, as if each leaf,
stone, and tree had a secret shimmering inside it.

"Eating" was next. Rosemary hesitated. Fact-
finding meant Exploring All Avenues, but what if
being scientific led you smack in the wrong direction? Away from comfortable facts. Smack into
. . . well, *magic*.

Impossible. Perhaps the herb of time simply
muddled one's internal clock. Rosemary wasn't
perfectly sure what her internal clock was, only
that her father's was always out of kilter for several
days after a long airplane trip. You *knew* what
o'clock it was here, but your insides were still
running on there-time.

Just one leaf. A pinch, a quick swallow, and it
was done. Rosemary held her breath.

Her stomach felt a bit . . . fizzy. For a moment
that was all. Then, by degrees, the bees' buzz rose
a note, and the birds' song became a twitter. Parsley sat almost motionless on the other side of the
bush, but his whiskers twitched at an alarming
rate.

Bees, birds, boughs, leaves, grass, and grasshop-
pers darted, twittered, rustled, and hopped in a
great and general rush. The garden stirred and
hummed at the treble, like a motion picture pro-
jected at high speed.

The shadow from the sundial moved too, like a

thin, dark finger across the TIME stone and the patch of time, tracing its way up the wall toward the great bronze sundial.

"Eating—gobbling up minutes," scribbled Rosemary.

But . . . oughtn't the shadow move *around* the dial? It crept straight up the wall. Perhaps it was not a dial for telling time at all. Or if it was, it must have been set in the wrong wall.

Rosemary looked at her watch. Almost three o'clock. It was suddenly almost three o'clock because the minute hand on the watch was moving almost as fast as if it were ticking off seconds. The finger of the shadow on the wall crept upward toward the dial and the six at its bottom.

No, toward the *three*. All the numbers were IIIs!

"But that's silly," said Rosemary crossly. Parsley Sage crept quietly into her lap, but she scarcely noticed. The hour hand on her watch and the shadow on the wall touched three at the same moment.

Rosemary, her scientific curiosity suddenly evaporated, rose and tried to run, but her feet were rooted to the stone.

For suddenly the sundial wasn't there.

Or the patch of wall behind it.

The woods were red and gold beyond the wall.

And two young people stood among the trees, staring at her, mouths agape.

The House
in the Woods

The girl wore a long, russet dress and no shoes. Her dark braids were wound around with brightly colored string, and she wore a knotted headband. She would have gone unnoticed in the shopping crowds at home on Wisconsin Avenue, but in the Maine woods the costume was oddly startling. Her companion might have drawn stares even in the city, not for his leather trousers or his own long braids or beaded moccasins, but for the quiver of arrows slung over his shoulder and the longbow that trembled in one hand.

"The Dreaming Trees!" he whispered.

"It is the sorceress's trick," the girl gasped. "Run!"

The girl leaped a patch of briars like a young

deer, disappearing in the direction of Bennickport village. The young man slipped through the pines and away northward.

Rosemary stood rooted for a long moment. One second the wall had been all-of-a-piece, and in the next there was a great gap. The two ancient elm trees, broad-branched and tall—yet somehow not so huge as she remembered—stood one at each side of the breach. Like thick towers, they rose to make a great, golden arch at the gate of a dark pine wood. Yellowing vines and glossy green laurels grew in the warm gloom, and wispy grass shone palely yellow in a noonday sun.

As Rosemary's panic faded, her curiosity grew like a mushroom. She approached the gap gingerly, hand outstretched. It went through quite easily, and she as easily after it.

The two great elms were definitely, solidly real, green with fine moss on the north side, and cool to the touch. Between them, just beneath Rosemary's feet, a faint trace of a path took up and wandered off into the wood.

Rosemary hesitated. But "not without a map and compass, dear" did not apply here. None of her mother's store of Good Advice applied to unexpected forests and upstart footpaths. Or to the unfamiliar excitement that brushed aside Rosemary's customary caution. Paths were for following.

Rosemary had gone no further than one step beyond the elms when behind her she heard a quiet *snick!* as if a door had closed. *As if a door had closed.*

She looked behind and almost shrieked. A grove of golden elms and red-leaved maples stood where Wychwood and its tangled garden should have been. Elms and maples, a tidy pigpen, and a neat log house, perhaps half as tall again as Rosemary.

"Oh, *come* now!" Rosemary objected. In a rush of panic she circled the trees twice and then stopped still in an absolute muddle.

The strange house was broad and long enough. It was simply—and alarmingly—squat. As if it had been made by—and for—dwarfs. Rosemary was as tall as the door.

"There's no such thing," said Rosemary sternly. And then she remembered uncomfortably that there really were such things as dwarfs, and that they weren't in the least magic. Real dwarfs were odd-sized ordinary people who lived in ordinary houses and worked at ordinary jobs. Unless they worked for circuses. Then they lived in trailers. But somehow all that seemed even odder than old tales of dwarf-miners living in wooden houses deep in misty mountain forests. Rosemary was distinctly confused. And Rosemary was not used to being confused.

As for what had happened to the garden wall,

why—the sundial part of it might have swung open like a door. Rosemary tried not to think about the worrisome fact that the back side of the wall was nowhere to be seen. There was no sense to be made of that at all.

Nonsensical. Of course, it only *seemed* nonsensical. So did a puzzle-game until you found the key. Rosemary took a long, shaky breath, and after a moment allowed herself a small smile of satisfaction. Aunt Sibby thought her dreadfully prim and proper, and Mother thought her delightfully so. Well, just this once she was going to give in to curiosity and snoop. The pigpen and the squatty house were better than a puzzle-game.

The minute Rosemary strode out from under the trees, the little white sow and five small piglets let out a chorus of squeals. As she came closer, they crowded into the far corner of the pen, one wedge of pig glaring out of six suspicious pairs of eyes. "*Stranger!*" they squealed again in unison—or something to that effect.

"Susannah? What *is* it?" came a quaver from inside the squatty house.

A pale blur moved behind a window patched together out of bits of bottle glass. There was the sound of fumbling with a latch, and the window swung out to show a little old lady with a face puckered up like an apple doll's and a small pink mouth drawn up in an O of surprise.

"Law, *another* one! Well, it just won't do," said the old lady pettishly. "One's enough. You'll have to fend for yourself. Your little friend's gone off yonder not five minutes ago. Well, fifteen or twenty, perhaps." She fluttered a hand off easterly. "Get along. I've enough worry with one. Three's two too many. Good-bye!"

The patchwork window slammed shut.

Snort, said Susannah the pig, looking smug.

Baba

"Three *what?*" called Rosemary, knocking on the door. "What friend? And who've you got in there? It's not Parsley, is it? Have you got my aunt's cat?" She banged harder and peered in the tiny door-window, but it was quite dark inside, and there was no answer.

Where *had* Parsley got to? He had been in her lap just before it happened.

"I can't have lost him! What will Aunt Sibby say? Pars*ley?* Parsley Cat?" Rosemary circled the cabin, calling. There was no sign of the old cat.

"Oh, *please* be back in the garden," she prayed. For there was really no way he could have got into the little cabin without her seeing.

"Excuse me," called Rosemary, tapping on the

door more politely this time. "Who did you say was here five minutes ago?"

Still no answer.

Rosemary looked at her watch, then took it off and shook it. It had stopped at three o'clock. How was she to know when it was getting close to suppertime? There was company coming, and that meant a bath and dressing up.

It also meant that there was no time to waste in knocking at unfriendly doors. The path the old lady had waved at wandered over a hummock and down through a stand of pumpkin pines. Rosemary set off feeling oddly cheerful.

To her surprise, on the other side of the hummock a large tortoiseshell cat sat waiting.

"*There* you are," scolded Rosemary. "Why didn't you come when I called. Thank goodness you're . . . Oh! *Are* you Parsley?" The cat's markings were much like Parsley's, but the longer she looked, the surer Rosemary was that it was not he.

This was a younger and heavier cat, satin-smooth and sleek-tailed. He stared back coolly, then turned, and trotted down the leaf-strewn path out of sight. Rosemary had the distinct impression, as strong as it was absurd, that he had ordered her to follow.

The pines along the way dwindled to scrub, and the forest leaf-carpet gave way to knee-deep, straggly grass. Beyond lay the Atlantic Ocean.

Rosemary walked down to the rocks above the water's edge and looked up and down the zigzag of the coastline. There wasn't even a proper beach like Rehoboth or the Cape. Not even a lighthouse. Only the young Parsley-cat perched on the nearest boulder.

"I could have walked down here any time," Rosemary grumbled at him. "Fifteen minutes for nothing."

"Who's there?" said a voice out of nowhere.

Rosemary jumped. At home, life went on for *weeks* without a surprise or a loud noise, but this afternoon looked like making up for ten years all at once. She drew a deep breath.

The voice had been a child's voice. And something about it . . . Rosemary forgot her customary caution and clambered out over the rocks. "Where are you?"

"Down here," said the voice, not very helpfully. Then a small hand raised up and waggled.

Rosemary scrambled toward the waggle, but slowed halfway there. A horrid thought had popped into her usually sensible head. What if it *wasn't* a child? It was a very un-Rosemary thought, and common sense bustled in to sweep it away. What could it be *but* a child? Mermaids did not exist. What olden sailors thought were mermaids were really sea cows, she told herself. And sea cows had flippers, not hands with fingers. She climbed further down.

A small, dark-haired girl sat in a hollow at the water's edge with the big cat draped across her lap. She was dressed, like Rosemary, in blue jeans, a striped T-shirt, and tennis shoes, but they were as filthy as if she had slept in the odd old woman's pigpen. She looked small for eight, but old for seven. And she had been crying, to judge from the grimy smears below her eyes. Rosemary felt oddly disappointed that she was no more outlandish than the seacoast.

"I'm Baba," the small girl offered, producing a smeary, timid smile. "I like your cat. Mine's just like him, but he's only a kitten. I lost him yesterday." She sniffled.

"I'm Rosemary Walpole," said Rosemary, "and he's not mine. 'Baba.' Is that short for Barbara? Barbara what?"

Baba frowned. "Barbara Sage. Actually it's Baba from Hepsibah, but I *hate* Hepsibah."

"It is pretty awful," Rosemary agreed.

"I'm glad you came," confided Baba. "Because I can't figure out what year we're in. You—you wouldn't have a sandwich, would you? I didn't think so. I mean, your pockets aren't big enough."

Rosemary's eye was on a sail that had just appeared on the horizon. "What year?" she echoed vaguely. "It's this year. What do you mean, 'What year'?"

Baba's brows were drawn together in concentration. "I forget what year the first Thanksgiving was. It must be after that, because Carolanna told Goody Cakebread she ought to send two piglets to the Squire's for the Thanksgiving feast, instead of one, like last year." Baba sighed, either out of pity for the piglets or a horrid yearning for a taste of one. "How about raisins?" she asked hopefully.

"Some people carry raisins in their pockets."

Rosemary was not really listening. The sailing ship—it was oddly tall and chunky for a yacht—was coming in on a southwesterly course that would take it well past the rocky headland and on down the coast. It was probably too large for the estuary at Bennickport, which, so far as she had seen the day before, harbored a small fishing fleet and a neat little pleasure marina. Squint as she might, Rosemary saw a three-masted schooner flying the British Union Jack, which seemed a little odd.

"Who," she said, still squinting, "is Goody Cakebread? And Carolanna."

Baba, her mind still on food, sighed and scratched

the cat delicately under the chin. "I didn't really think you'd have any. Well, Carolanna's the preacher's slave. She's an Indian. Goody Cakebread says she's from down in Carolina, so she's named after where she's from. Goody Cakebread said I mustn't let her see me because she's a Trouble-maker."

At "preacher's slave," Rosemary had blinked and begun to listen. She stared, fascinated. Baba was absolutely batty. "Goody Cakebread—is she the old lady back in the woods?"

Baba nodded. "That's right. The old witch."

To the Rescue

Rosemary blinked again, the ship forgotten.

"A witch? You're just saying that," she said disapprovingly. The old lady was odd and her house even odder, but that only made her what Mother humorously called "a New England Original."

"No, really," Baba insisted. "Carolanna asked her if she was keeping the baby to cook up in a batch of witches' flying ointment, and it made Goody Cakebread dreadfully angry. She said sometimes girls' noses drop off from too much sticking them in other people's business. That was when Carolanna ran off."

"What does that prove?" Rosemary tried hard not to appear interested in such absurdities. "*What* baby?"

Baba considered. She gave a lopsided shrug. "Well, not a baby, exactly. I mean, he can walk and talk, sort of. I think his name is Wim."

Rosemary sighed. Baba's explanation needed explanations. "Look, er—Baba. Maybe we'd better go back there. And while we're going, why don't you tell me everything from the beginning?"

"Okay." Baba shoved the cat from her lap and scrambled up out of her hollow. "*I* got here yesterday," she said. "It was nice for a while. I played in the woods. But at suppertime I couldn't find my way home, so I knocked on her door. Goody Cakebread's, I mean. It was funny. She pretended to be scared of me." Talking all the while, Baba followed Rosemary up across the rocks and into the dry grass.

"Anyhow, she let me in and gave me cider and some biscuity cookies with nuts in." Baba paused.

"And?" prodded Rosemary.

Baba gave another of her one-shoulder shrugs. "Then I said, 'Thank you,' and asked her the way home, but she got all twittered and said how should she know? I had to go away, she said. She got sort of screechy. So I went. But only just a little way, because it was getting dark. After a bit I came back and slept with the pigs."

She giggled. "They were squirmy. And that Susannah-pig didn't like it much, until she figured I made them warmer too."

Rosemary was impressed. Being warm *was* worth being dirty. "But what about the baby?"

Baba had to half-run to keep up. "That was this morning," she panted. "He was just *there*. Outside the pigpen, crying. He kept saying, 'Doggy-doggy,' when he wasn't crying. Maybe he never saw a pig before. . . . That's when the witch came out," she added hastily, as Rosemary turned with an impatient scowl. "She was even upsetter than before."

The baby had cried, Goody Cakebread had fussed, and Baba had refused to budge until the old woman showed her the way home. The baby won. "I guess all sorts of old ladies like babies," said Baba. "Even witches. We got cornmeal mush and honey and tea and bacon for breakfast, and she jiggled Wim on her knee, and he called her 'Gan-ma.' I had two bowls of cornmeal mush with honey," she said wistfully.

"Carol*anna*," prompted the unsympathetic Rosemary.

"Oh. *That*'s when I knew she was a witch," said Baba dramatically. "Because this girl knocked on the door, you see, and called out that Mistress Grout had sent her for the piglets. So I had to go under the bed. She stuck Wim in the cupboard. And it's a very peculiar cupboard. . . ."

Carolanna had leaned in at the door, fearful of

coming farther. She was in far enough, however, to hear the bumping in the cupboard and see the roly-poly white piglet that tumbled out when the door bumped open.

"I take that one, Goodwife Cakebread," she announced. "Mist'ess say I bring fattest two."

"No, no, not this one," dithered the old woman. She flapped her skirts to drive the piglet back into the cupboard. "It's my own dear piglet and not for eating."

Carolanna shrugged. "Ah, well. Mist'ess never know." She smiled shyly. "He very nice pig. What his name?"

"Wim," said Goody Cakebread primly as she closed the cupboard door. Baba, under the bed, clapped both hands over her mouth to stifle an astonished squeak.

"He want out bad," Carolanna observed blandly as the door bumped open again. "Why you keep him in cupboard? . . . *Aiee!*" She shrieked, for this time Wim the baby tumbled out.

And there was no piglet to be seen.

"And he's still there? Shut up in a cupboard with a pig? That's . . . that's Child Abuse!" sputtered Rosemary indignantly. At Baba's blank look, she explained, "That's cruelty to children. Of course, she's not a *witch*. There's no such thing. Could she be crazy? That must be it. She must be crazy.

We'll have to rescue him. Even if I'm late to dinner."

Baba's eyes shone. When she was excited, they
grew round as saucers. "Okay. How?"

Baba, Rosemary suspected, had visions of stuff-
ing her old witch in her oven. "I haven't decided
yet," said Rosemary, walking even faster.

They were deep in the elm wood before Rosemary thought to ask, "Why wouldn't she tell you
how to get home? Where did you come from?"

"Wychwood," said Baba.

Old Bennickport

As a witch, Goody Cakebread proved a great disappointment. Rosemary had called in at the window, "Don't you *dare* hurt that baby. And we won't go away until you give him to us." At which Baba had shrieked, "Yes, we *will* go away, and we'll bring all the king's men to arrest you."

"All the king's men," muttered Rosemary. "Honestly!"

But then came the sound of the door being hastily unbarred.

"The Lord be praised, here you are. I never wanted him in the first place. I've had strange visitors before . . ."

A little, white-haired, bosomy woman in a long gray dress appeared in the doorway to shoo out a small, curly-headed boy, flapping her apron after him as she talked, as if he were a straying piglet. She then proceeded to make a great fuss over the tortoiseshell cat, calling it Tiddy Dumpling, and Bad Cat, finally snatching it up, whisking inside, and slamming and barring the door. Behind it, they heard her crooning, "Oliver Tolliver, where have you *been*?"

Oliver *Tolliver*?

"You were wonderful," panted a saucer-eyed Baba, trotting behind Rosemary, who carried Wim. "I was sure she'd turn you into a mouse or a toad or something."

"She couldn't, silly." Rosemary laughed. She staggered a little under the weight of the very husky Wim, and after another few yards, she stopped.

"It must be *miles* to Bennickport. This *has* to be the road I came in on yesterday. My aunt said it was the only way. So we should've passed the Playhouse by now. Little boy, how would you like to do some walking on your own two feet?"

"I walk *dood*," Wim said. "To Witswood."

"You do that," said Rosemary sourly. *Had* both of them really come by way of Wychwood? She wondered if Aunt Sibby knew that the neighborhood children made so free with her garden. She fiddled nervously with her watch. It still refused to move past three o'clock. She followed Wim slowly, twisting at the winding-stem.

"What d'you suppose Goody Cakebread meant? You know—just before she saw her old cat. About how we ought to know our way home because the others always did?"

"Who knows?" said Rosemary airily. "Old people talk like that." Privately, she had to admit that it puzzled her too. What the old woman had said was, "I've had strange visitors before, but after a cup of cider and a nice talk, they disappeared right back into thin air where they come from, 'thout any trouble. They knew their way home. 'Course, none of them were children, neither," she had added sourly.

Rosemary caught up with Wim and took his hand. "What's important," she said impressively, "is restoring this Poor Child to his Grieving Parents." If she was disappointed that her adventure was proving only mildly nonsensical, she managed not to show it. But she did spoil the effect a little by adding, "Before time for my bath."

Baba's doubtful look returned. If, as Rosemary insisted, they weren't walking around in Pilgrim times, why hadn't Goody Cakebread had a car? Or at least a bicycle. But Rosemary was very sure.

Actually, Rosemary had only seemed positive. For if it was the twenty-first of June, 1975, it was a very odd June that insisted on looking and feeling like November. And going sweaterless in the chilly sunshine produced some very realistic shivers.

The obvious answer was that it was all a dream. What better explanation for openings in walls and not being able to find the way back through? If only everything weren't so uncomfortably solid— including the landscape. In dreams, one place simply dissolved into another. You didn't have to get tired and dusty trudging from here to there. Rosemary shivered again.

Around yet another of the many bends in the dusty road—somehow she had missed noticing yesterday that it was really little more than a rutted track—they came upon a shed and a cow. Beyond, past a patch of corn and behind a tidy picket fence, a dog stood on the doorstep of a small shingled house and barked at them. As they passed, he dashed out and ran yapping along the fence after them. There was no one in sight, either at that first house, or the next they came to, or its barn.

The rutted dirt road became first a lane, running between neat fields and pastures and kitchen gardens, and then an unpaved street lined with young elms. There was still not a soul in sight. On one clothesline, two long aprons and an embroidered petticoat flapped alongside, of all things, an old-fashioned man's nightshirt.

"Where *is* everybody?" Rosemary asked nervously. She and Baba dragged a tired and hungry Wim between them. "This isn't the way I came yesterday at all. What is this place?"

"I'm not sure," hedged Baba. "I *think* it's Bennickport. Those houses look an awful lot like the ones along by the village library. Only they're . . . newer. And the trees are different."

Rosemary opened her mouth to protest. It stayed open in amazement. Away to the left, a bell had begun to toll, and out the front door of the house farthest along the street hurried a lady in long, gray skirts, a ruffled white collar and cuffs, and a neat white bonnet-cap. The man who followed wore a long-skirted jacket and a tall hat. They were around the corner in a moment and out of sight.

"Oh *dear*," said Rosemary, her heart sinking. Whatever they were dressed for, it was not 1975. They looked uncomfortably like the stiff, frowning figures of the old engravings in Aunt Sibby's book, *Bennickport in the Early Years*.

"It could be an Olden Days festival, and everybody has to dress up. Maybe my aunt just forgot to tell me about it," she added lamely.

Baba shook her head. "Down in York they have Old York Days, but Bennickport doesn't. Besides, why would Goody Cakebread get dressed up like that just for staying at home? *I* think we got magicked back into the Pilgrim days."

"No, this isn't Bennickport," said Rosemary desperately, refusing to listen. "We just took the wrong road."

"It was the only one there was," Baba pointed out.

"It was just the first one we *came* to," said Rosemary, grabbing at a straw.

Wim sniffled. "I cold. I wanna go home." He sat down in a drift of yellow leaves and dust and gave Rosemary a mulish look. "Now."

"We'll have to turn him in at the Meeting House," puffed Rosemary, dragging at his arm. Wim in a cupboard might be an adventure, but Wim Rescued was a distinct nuisance. "Somebody'll know where he belongs. Then we can go back and try again for the right road."

Baba snatched at Wim's other hand and hung on fiercely. "*No.* What if that Preacher Grout's there? Goody Cakebread says he's *mean.*" She was close to tears. "He told Carolanna next time she ran away he'd have a *G* burned on her cheeks so everybody everywhere'd know she belonged to him."

She faltered. "I suppose he couldn't really do it, even if we are in the olden days, but it was a mean thing to say."

For once Rosemary did not argue. She was no longer absolutely positively sure of anything but the cold and that her feet hurt. And she was frightened. But how could Baba be right? How *could* they be back in early New England? She had only stepped over the patch of time and through what must have been a door in the garden wall. . . .

Stepped over a patch of time . . .

Oh, dear.

Certainly not everything could be explained away as easily as the sailing ship (a replica, like the *Mayflower II*, she had decided) or the "costumes." Tire tracks were as missing in the dusty streets as the cars that should have made them. Back at the side of the house where they now stood, a horse stamped and nickered in what ought to have been a garage. And Parson Grout's threat might not have been so empty. Rosemary knew from social studies class that people did do dreadful things to slaves.

She dithered for a minute, bit her lip, and then gave in. "Okay. If you're right, we'll keep him. But there's not much time to find out if we've got to backtrack all that way—"

"Listen," Baba hissed. "*Listen!*" Her eyes were round as saucers.

The sound of voices singing rose in the sharp, clear air, coming from somewhere not far off. The tune was slow and dreary, and the words at times blurred together, but the girls could make out some of it. *For, lo, the wicked bend their bow. (Tum-tum-tumty) their arrow upon the string, that they may (tum-tiddity) shoot at the upright in heart.*

It sounded more ominous than churchy. After a bit there was a voice speaking, then a long silence.

Rosemary shook little Wim, who had curled up and gone to sleep on his pile of leaves. "Wake up, you silly thing. Time for a piggyback ride."

With Wim aboard, Rosemary still wavered. Back or forward? "There isn't *time*," she fretted. "It must be nearly five. But—well, remember: just a *peek*."

At the corner, the cross street curved dustily downhill to meet the leaf-littered village green. A large crowd stood patiently on the far side, in the road in front of the odd four-gabled meeting-house, which Rosemary, with a sinking feeling, recognized. Aunt Sibby had whizzed past it in the Lotus with the remark, "Behold the Ark! Oldest church in Maine."

Some in the crowd were talking quietly. All kept an eye on the church door. Everyone, old and young, was dressed like a figure in an old painting. Here and there along the street a horse was tethered to a tree, and below the little green a number of wagons lined the road to the river bridge.

Rosemary jiggled Wim nervously. How could she be *sure*? With a cautious beckoning gesture to Baba, she slipped from the shelter of one tree to the next and the next again. They reached an old giant of a beech at the near edge of the green at the moment a gaunt, black-garbed figure appeared in the meeting-house doorway.

"That's Parson Grout. I just *know* it is," Baba whispered.

Rosemary nodded.

A dozen or so grim-faced men followed the tall man out onto the broad steps. Most joined the crowd in the road. One—a stocky, uncomfortable-looking gentleman in brown—stood at the gaunt man's elbow.

"Dear friends," boomed the parson somberly—for it must be Parson Grout—"your selectmen and elders are cautious men, wishing to think well of an old neighbor, but they have come at last to agree with me. The woman Cakebread is indeed a witch and must be brought to trial before she puts us all in peril.

"We have heard this day a witness to the witch's traffic with the devil's imps. She conjures imps with hair of flames out of the very air. She has about her a familiar spirit in the shape of a great cat, and has a pig that she transforms at will into the shape of a human babe. She . . ."

There were gasps from the crowd. Rosemary and Baba looked at each other in horror.

"That does it." Rosemary jiggled the sleepy child on her back, shifting him higher. "You first," she hissed at Baba. She jerked her head in the direction from which they had come.

The catalog of Goody Cakebread's mischiefs was still being recited as they breasted the hill. Below, the crowd groaned and muttered like a tormented dog straining at its leash.

Too Late

"*Me?*" Goody Cakebread gasped, clapping a hand to her heart. "Accused for a witch? Oh dear, oh dear, oh dear! And to think my Goodman warned me to be wary of the parson, and I paid no heed."

Goody Cakebread and the wheeled cart she used for collecting firewood had been fetched by Baba, who had run on ahead. Wim bounced along in the cart behind Baba and the old lady, howling in protest at every bump. Rosemary, exhausted from carrying him so far, stumbled behind.

"Hush, hush, child," warned the old lady. She took up her cart rope again. "If 'twere heard, anyone would say your caterwauling comes of my sticking you with pins. Do hush!"

Wim did hush—so abruptly that Baba snapped,

"She didn't say she *would* stick you with pins, you baby. Only that you sounded like it."

Rosemary's voice was still a wheeze, but she managed to ask, "Why do they call you 'Goody' if they think you're so dreadful?"

The old lady looked more stricken than before. "It means only 'Goodwife,' being not so polite as 'Mistress.' Where can you be from that you do not know that? No, no! Best not tell me. I fear to know."

Rosemary frowned. Whatever Goody Cakebread was, it was not a witch.

When they reached the path to Goody Cake-bread's house, the narrow cart bumped so wildly that Wim was set down to walk. The old lady led the way, and when she came to the two great elm trees, she followed the well-worn path around the left-hand one instead of the fainter path that led directly between the two. Rosemary dimly noticed the detour, but thought it no odder than anything else. There were more important things to think of.

Like getting back to Wychwood, late for dinner or not.

And explaining Baba and Wim when she got there.

Goody Cakebread pushed open her low door and stepped down into a dim, low-beamed room warmed by a tiny fire in a wide stone fireplace. Rosemary saw why the little house had looked so oddly squatty: it was little more than a cellar with a roof on. In the corner nearest the fireplace, a low bed with a puffy mattress stood with a battered leather trunk at its foot. There was a table with some covered dishes, a rocker, an old carved oak "press" cupboard with two doors above and two below, and that was all—except for the pots and herbs hanging from the beams and a few odd dishes and cups on the mantel.

"Oliver? Oliver! Dear me, that cat's off again." Goody Cakebread hurried to the trunk and began to root in it.

"Where are you going to go?" asked Rosemary.

"Up to the Saco Valley to my friends the Soko-kis," the old lady answered. She stuffed a night-gown, warm hose, and three woolen petticoats into a pillow case.

"The So-kokeys? Who are they?"

"Indians, of course. The Sokokis aren't fair-weather friends, like some." She sniffed. "When my dear Miller Cakebread was alive and we lived in a wide house by the mill, Bennickport was glad enough of us. But be a widow and poor, with a son run off to sea . . . Ah, well, as the miller used to say, 'Be wise and fret not, be virtuous and regret naught.'" She dropped a pair of heeled shoes with fine tortoiseshell buckles back into the trunk. "I shan't be needing those in the woods."

"I was sort of thinking," said Rosemary casually, "that maybe we ought to come with you."

"In for a penny, in for a pound?" asked Goody Cakebread shrewdly.

Baba almost dropped the biscuit she was buttering for Wim. "Honestly? To live with the Indians?"

"Only till we find out how to get home," said Rosemary hastily.

Goody Cakebread nodded. "I think 'tis a wise thought. Gunty Ramanoke knows the dwellings in these woods better than any white man in the province of Maine. If this house you come from . . ." She fluttered her hand nervously. "If it *be* from some other here-and-now, so to speak, perhaps he will know of that too. Gunty Ramanoke is the great *m'téoulin* of the Sokokis."

"Um-tee-what?"

"*M'téoulin.* 'Tis their word for a great worker of—magic." Goody Cakebread fidgeted as if the very word made her nervous. She bustled over to the carved cupboard standing in the dim far corner. "I do mislike leaving this," she sighed. "My Goodman's granny said 'twas the family's fortune, and ill luck would come of being rid of it. Perhaps Gunty Ramanoke's sons can come one night and fetch it up to the Saco."

Opening the upper left-hand door she drew out a sausage-shaped bundle. Unrolled on the bed, it turned out to be two middling-size brown gowns with white collars, two tie-string caps, a small tan smock with little woolen leggings to go under, and three pairs of buckled shoes.

Baba crowed. "I *told* you it was a magic cupboard!"

"Oh, hush, child!" cried Goody Cakebread, dashing to the window to peer out down the path. "Hush, do, and put them on. Your own shirts are so brightly striped they could be seen a mile away in the wood." Under her breath she added, "And pantaloons on girl-children! Tush!"

The clothes were a perfect fit. While Rosemary buttoned Wim up, the old lady bundled the T-shirts and jeans into a roll, and stuffed them in the top of the cupboard. Opening the lower doors, she drew out a large wicker basket, packed full, with a neat white napkin over the top.

"Our supper." The old lady popped up and out the door too quickly for questions.

Far off, the village dogs barked and bayed.

"Come, come," urged Goody Cakebread.

The wagon scarcely held it all: supper, Wim, the pillowcase bundle, and the five piglets. Susannah, tied to the back end, had to make the Saco Valley on her own trotters.

Or would have had to.

Rosemary and Baba, pulling the wagon, followed Goody Cakebread along a little-used thread of a path. They had barely passed from the elm grove into the pines when the first dog caught up, attacking Susannah from the rear. Enraged, Susannah turned to fight.

And tipped the wagon over. The path was a shambles of pigs, dogs, and shrieks.

The villagers were not far behind.

There was nothing to be done. The fugitives watched the piglets being rounded up. Solemnly, the town marshall read out his warrant. Reverend Thanatopsis Grout glared in triumph, but everyone else looked away and shuffled their feet, suddenly embarrassed.

Two wagons were brought up and the little party of prisoners was escorted out to the wagon track to be loaded up. And the Town Clerk scribbled dutifully in his notebook that "Goodwife Cakebread, three Imps of the Devil, six piglike Familiars, and one reputed wizard's cupboard from said Cakebread's house [One familiar Catt missing] removed to York Gaol."

Old York Gaol

As jails go, York Gaol, which served the whole of York County and, therefore, Bennickport, was more like a sparsely furnished house. Goody Cakebread's bed was almost as comfortable as her own at home, and the children, though they had to sleep on the floor, had ticking pallets well stuffed with straw. As beds go, they were soft enough, but noisy.

There were blankets in plenty and a new candle in a tin holder, for though Preacher Grout maintained that the Devil Could Warm His Own, and though Mistress Grout warned that a candle might be made to burn down a jail, the jailer's wife hid a soft heart under her rasping manner. She loved children ("Imps of the Devil, my foot!"), and she was also an excellent cook.

Goody Cakebread's lowered spirits and her concern for the missing Oliver Tolliver did not prevent her polishing off half a chicken, three gravy-soaked pieces of bread, a bowl of green-bean salad, and a wedge of pumpkin pie. " 'Tis a pity," said she, daintily licking her fingers before wiping them on her apron, "that they've not locked my dear cupboard up with us."

Rosemary, adding the remains of a chicken wing to her pile of bones, looked up warily. "Why? It's empty. Our old clothes weren't even in it when the marshall looked. We were lucky you got rid of them."

"Oh, but *I* didn't," said Goody Cakebread. Her smile crinkled her cheeks. "It did. The cupboard."

"It *is* magic," whispered a wide-eyed Baba, ignoring a scornful sniff from Rosemary.

Goody Cakebread tiptoed to the door. She listened for a long moment to be sure the jailer and his wife were still downstairs with the men from Bennickport.

"It would be ill luck indeed if the tale came to the wrong ears," whispered the old lady. She tiptoed back to her bed. "Forty years ago that cupboard and Oliver Tolliver were wedding gifts to the miller and me from his dear granny. Granny was . . . well, odd. The more years I think on it, the odder it seems she was."

"But—" put in Rosemary with a frown, "Oliver Tolliver can't be forty."

"Oh?" Goody Cakebread seemed confused by the interruption. "No, of course he couldn't be, could he? Granny's would have been the *first* Oliver Tolliver."

She took up the thread of her story again. "That was in the old country, and when Miller Cakebread set his heart on leaving Lancashire for the New World, we took the cupboard to pieces and packed it in a stout wood box and brought it along with our bits of china and good spool chairs. It was a year until our mill was built in Bennickport, another until our house was finished and the last box unpacked, and half another before we discovered that the cupboard was even odder than Granny."

Rosemary forgot that she was being skeptical. "How? What did it do?"

"We began to miss things," whispered Goody Cakebread. "Always things we had no need for: gloves without mates, saucers without cups, a cracked tureen . . . Then one day, as I went to put away the fresh-ironed sheets, I thought, 'These be so much-mended, we'll be needing new, soon's we've put by a bit of silver.' And—and when I opened the cupboard, there were six fine linen sheets fit for the Queen herself!"

"And the next time you looked, the old ones

were gone?" prompted Baba breathlessly. The old lady nodded.

Rat-tat.

The sharp knock at the door made them all jump. After the sound of the sliding bar came the scritch of a key in the lock. Only Wim, full of pie and curled up on his pallet, was not alarmed. He burrowed deeper under his blanket as the opening door let in a draft of air.

Parson Grout stood glowering in the doorway. Behind him, the landing was crowded with stern-faced men whose shadows dipped and swayed in the flickering light of the jailer's candle.

"Bring down the smallest female first," snapped the parson. He turned on his heel.

The jailer reassured Baba. " 'Tis only to take a deposition—to write down an account of yourself and your dealings with Widow Cakebread. Don't be frighted."

"That's right." The marshall, a gruff, hearty man named Hobbs, nodded in agreement. "Just a formality. The real examinations must wait for judge and jury. 'Tisn't like the old days, you know, Mistress Cakebread. It's been twenty, thirty years since there been any witches hanged or pressed." He backed out apologetically, locking the door behind him.

"The cupboard! It doesn't work for everyone,

does it?" asked Rosemary, trying hard not to think what Baba's too-ready tongue might be tripping over downstairs. "Old Preacher Pickle-Face would have loved to find it full of dried bats and toads and witches' recipe books, but it didn't give him *his* wish."

The old lady nodded. "Miller Cakebread always said, 'It knows to whom it belongs.' And 'tis a very wise and cautious cupboard, for it only answers need, not greed. Once I thought to ask it for new bed-curtains." The old lady chortled softly. "It gave me a tablet of soap to wash the old ones, for they were perfectly good."

Rosemary smiled wanly.

Mr. Hobbs brought Baba back at last, and beckoned Rosemary to follow next. Goody Cakebread had braided her hair into two fat plaits ("So's you don't look so odd and wild," the old lady said), and Rosemary tried to concentrate on keeping her hands folded and looking prim. It should not have been difficult, for she had spent much of her ten years looking prim. Now it felt oddly absurd.

Rosemary was taken down to the sparely furnished front room to face the preacher, sprawled in a wing chair like a long-legged black spider. There were more curious observers than there were chairs and benches, and a few of the men watched the preacher with sharp, unfriendly frowns.

"Heaven hears you, Rose Mary Walpole," warned Mr. Grout dramatically. "And Andrew Wiggleton, the Bennickport Town Clerk, will take down all you say, so have a care for the truth. Now: what are your parents' names?"

All of the questions were like that, and not a one about Goody Cakebread. If answering was like filling out a school questionnaire, it was also full of hidden pitfalls.

"Where is your father's home?" (Stretching a point, she said Salem. Washington might not exist yet.)

"How came you to Bennickport?" (By carriage. After all, the Lotus *was* a horseless carriage.)

And so on. Rosemary had a wicked urge to mention that she had flown as far as Boston, just to see their faces. She managed to resist it. With every mild answer, she saw that the preacher's temper grew more frayed.

"What then brought you to Goodwife Cakebread's?" asked Mr. Grout at last, darkly, drumming his fingers on a bony knee.

"I was lost, please, sir," answered Rosemary meekly. "I wandered off and couldn't find the way back to my Aunt Walpole's house."

"Take the brat away," snapped the preacher. "Bring Goodwife Cakebread."

"Of *course*, I didn't let on we don't belong in

their old Bennickport." Baba was offended. "I told them my name was Hepsibah Walpole, and my father's house was north of their old town."

"Now why'd you say *that*?" wailed Rosemary. "What did they say?"

Baba shrugged lop-sidedly. "They said, 'How far north?' and I said I didn't exactly know."

"I don't mean about that. I mean . . . oh, never mind!" Rosemary paced up and down before the window. Perhaps it wasn't such a bad idea. Parson Grout and the others would suppose they were cousins; that Baba's mother was Rosemary's aunt.

"Anyhow, I found out where the cupboard is, and where they put the pigs," Baba announced. She helped herself to the last sliver of pie in the pie-dish. "I just asked. Do you know, they put the pigs in the *dungeon*? There's really a dungeon, and they really put them there."

"Only until Mistress Grout gets her hands on them, I bet. Then all they'll be is smoked bacon and roast piglet." Rosemary, at the window, cupped her hands beside her eyes to shut out reflections, and stared out into the darkness. "For Pete's sake Baba? *Ssst!*" she hissed. "Someone's out there in the tree."

It was Carolanna.

Baba was at the window in a flash. "What's she up a tree for?"

"How should I know? To see how good a fix

she's got us into with her tattling, I suppose."

The figure in the tree gestured urgently.

"But we can't get out that way. Can't she see there's bars?" Baba shook her head violently and pointed.

Rosemary was fumbling the window-catch open. She was able to pull the sash up far enough to call out softly, "What do you want? And be *quiet*. If Parson Grout looks out the window . . ."

The girl sniffled as if she had been crying. "Oh, please, young mist'ess, my friend Gunty, his father Gunty Ramanoke tell him I am witless turkey hen to think Mist'ess Cakebread a witch and you bad spirits. He say you real as real. And my friend, he say he want no waggle-tongue for wife, so now I got no place to run away to when I run away." She snuffled and hiccuped together.

Baba giggled in spite of herself. Rosemary elbowed her in the ribs.

"So?"

"So," said Carolanna tragically, "I must undo all my doing, don't I?"

"*How?*"

Carolanna clung to her branch, looking very small. "I—I didn't thought that far," she faltered.

Out and Away

"Are there bars, dear?" Goody Cakebread called softly out the open window. "*Are-there-bars-on-the-storeroom-dear?*" Because of the bars on their own window, she could not lean out far enough to see where Carolanna had got to.

"No," came the soft answer.

There was the scraping squeak of a long-unopened window sash, a pause, and then a frightened whisper. "The cupboard is here. Truly must I open it?"

"Yes, you silly goose." Goody Cakebread squeezed her eyes tight shut and thought of keys, files, rope ladders—of all sorts of things the cupboard might usefully produce. Parson Grout and the others had gone shortly after the depositions were taken, but there were still the jailer and his wife to hear. If the girl should make a noise . . .

Rosemary and Baba, listening at the door for a step on the stairs, kept their fingers crossed and heard nothing but the rustle of straw as Wim shifted on his pallet.

"Well?" hissed Goody Cakebread, as Carolanna reappeared below. "Was there nothing? Drat! Now she's gone again."

Carolanna was back in a few minutes with a short ladder borrowed, by its battered look, from somebody's stable. When she had climbed as near the upstairs window as she could get, she held up the heavy object that hung from a cord around her neck. "I find only this."

Goody Cakebread stuck the candle out between the bars, the better to see what it was.

It was a bottle. A large, squat-bottomed bottle, sealed with a fat blob of sealing wax and labeled *Apple Cordiall.*

Two hours later, at the meeting of the north road and the path east to the squatty house, Goody Cakebread, Carolanna, and the children met Oliver Tolliver, leading a small party of the Sokokis. Alarmed at the appearance of the cat without his mistress, the Sokokis had hurried down trail to spy out what had happened to their old friend. The Ramanokes, Old Gunty and Pala and young

Gunty, had come, along with three older men, a marvelously fat old woman, and six young men, who had been hoping for a bit of excitement.

The Sokokis greeted Goody Cakebread with affection and much good-natured joking about her unsuspected skill in witchcraft. They eyed the children with great curiosity.

"I do not understand," objected Gunty Ramanoke in the middle of the old lady's explanations. "How could this silly girl free you with a bottle of apple spirits?"

"It was really quite clever of Carolanna. Not at *all* turkey-witted." Goody Cakebread stroked a purring Oliver Tolliver and beamed at Carolanna, who stood at young Gunty's side. "At first we thought my dear cupboard had given up and sent me a farewell nip, so to speak. But then my young friends"—she nodded toward Rosemary and Baba— "My young friends pointed out that we could not have used a key to escape in any case, for our door was barred as well as locked, and to file our way out would have taken all night or longer. We needed friends inside: Carolanna and the bottle. Tell Gunty, my dear, what you did."

Carolanna, suddenly shy, covered her face as every head in the circle of Sokokis turned toward her, but at a nudge from young Gunty, she found her tongue.

"It was nothing. I knock on the door, like so, and

call to Mist'ess Jailer. She come quick and I tell her old Revvind Grout and Mist'ess Grout send gift for trouble they take with the witches. I say they staying at Revvind Sample's house in York, but tell me I must walk home to Bennickport. And I frightened in the dark for fear the witch send spirits to get me for my tattle-tongue."

Carolanna smiled behind her fingers. "Mist'ess Gaoler, she say, 'Come child, you sleep in store-room, go in morning.' After while I peek, see her take two glasses from kitchen, and in a little while again I see they both asleep and bottle nearly empty. So I take keys and let out Mist'ess Cake-bread and the children.

"Oh, I almost forgot. We bring this, too." Carol-anna passed a familiar bundle tied up in a T-shirt to Rosemary. "I find it in that cupboard when I pretend sleep in the storeroom. It was not there first time, but it is clothes I see on the children be-fore."

Old Gunty Ramanoke squatted, took out his pouch, and striking a spark from his flint into a pinch of finely shredded bark, nursed a light for his pipe. After a thoughtful puff or two he said to Carolanna, "They will know you have done this. You are not afraid?"

Carolanna clung to young Gunty.

The young man, embarrassed but proud, listened to her whisper, and then explained. "My Carol-

anna, she has knocked over many things in the storeroom, and dropped her torn headband, as if she had been taken against her will."

Rosemary almost blurted out, "That was *my* idea," but for once she thought twice. Facts could be distracting, as well as useful. It was a new thought.

But the old man had seen Rosemary lean forward and then think better of it. There was little that he missed. His eyes remained on her as he said softly, between puffs, "It will be wise for my son and his bride to leave tonight for a visit to the upriver Sokokis. Our good friend the Widow Cakebread will be safe in my lodge a little while, disguised as one of us. My wife Pala is of much the same size and can provide clothing. But what of these children?"

Old Gunty puffed again. "What do we do with these children who have fallen through a hole out of another world into our own?"

The circle fell very still in its astonishment. Nothing moved but the moonlight shimmering through the leaves.

Gunty Ramanoke's eye was still on Rosemary.

"Well," said she, swallowing nervously. "Could you tell us how to get home? I mean, not right this minute, but . . ."

"Yes," said Old Gunty Ramanoke. He closed his eyes and blew a large doughnut of smoke.

"Turn right, and walk one hundred paces."

The path to Goody Cakebread's lay at Rosemary's right hand.

Goody Cakebread's mouth was a little O of astonishment. "A hundred yards? But that's no farther than the elms you call your Dreaming Trees."

The Dreaming Trees

"Great Wuchowsen!" Young Gunty exclaimed. "May the devil Lox take me if I did not see it happen and still not understand. For I saw this child"—he indicated Rosemary—"step out of the thin air between the Dreaming Trees and walk to our friend Cakebread's house."

Goody Cakebread shook her head in wonder. "Dear me, is *that* where all my strange visitors pop out from?"

"I saw too," put in Carolanna excitedly. "But I thought it sorcery, like in the tale Gunty has told me of the sorcerer Pulowech and the men who pop out of rocks."

Baba, who hadn't said anything for a long while, now pleaded sleepily, "Please? Is it far? It's tired, and I'm cold." She had changed her back into her own clothes and, shivering, clutched the brown gown over her shoulders like a shawl.

"Go home Witswood," little Wim mumbled into Pala Ramanoke's large, soft bosom.

"Come, then." The old man rose and stepped softly down the path.

Rosemary came last, stopping a minute in the shadows to pull on her jeans and tug the warm dress off over her head. The cold T-shirt made her shiver, but she scuffed the buckle shoes off happily.

Yet with her tennis shoes tied, she still dawdled. Her worry about being late for dinner had dwindled to a pinprick. Now that the *m'téoulin* promised a way home, she realized how much she had looked forward to a night in an Indian lodge and an unpredictable tomorrow. Now she would probably never have either.

"Here," said Gunty Ramanoke. Reverently he touched the rough bark of one great bole with the palm of his hand. "Here is the gate you came through. On one day that is yet-to-come you stepped between these trees and fell into our time."

"Surely there is more to it than that, or folk would be popping through every day," said Goody Cakebread. She eyed the great elm trees warily. "I knew you'd some queer notion about keeping out from betwixt them—I always took your long way round myself—but I don't see as they're so special. Wych elms, that's all they are. There were wych elms in Lancashire when I was a girl."

Gunty Ramanoke grunted. "That may be. But these are not the elms of this country. The others, yes, but not these two. Their girth tells their great age. Each must be a good eighteen paces around. No Pilgrim Father set them here."

He smiled at that, but then his voice grew soft and the words came slowly, as if he drew them out of the deepest place within his heart.

"These trees were planted, children-yet-to-be, in the dark years before the Long Men peopled this land, and the Long Men held these shores and valleys in the age before the first Abenaki walked here. It was from the last of the Long Men that our fathers heard them named the Forbidden Trees. They had grown here from the Dawn-Time, they said, and were the gateway to the world of the Dead, for none returned who disappeared beyond them."

Rosemary trembled with the cold. "But you said we could go back," she whispered.

Gunty Ramanoke nodded but spun his tale his own way. "My grandfather's grandfather, the first Ramanoke, was a great *m'téoulin*. It was he who found that the Long Men were mistaken. One day he left his lodge on a journey to find a dreaming-place, where he might be alone and pray and fast for a vision. For wisdom comes in visions.

"On that day he was drawn to this place, and despite his fears, he set his feet upon the unused path. Between one heartbeat and the next he found himself in a strangely beautiful garden and at once sat himself down to consider. For though he wished to examine the strange lodge beyond the fence of tall bushes, and though he wished above all things to know more of the pale-skinned people who came and went there, he dared not. For it came to him that the way back was hedged about with a magic for which he had no key. To take one step into that world would be to stay there, and so from middle-morning until dusk he crouched on the rim of the two worlds, listening much and learning a little.

"Since that day it is forbidden for any but *m'téoulins* wise with years and skilled in visions to go there and watch. The young and foolish, curious and daring, would stray into that other time and be caught there, like fishes stranded in a meadow after a flood."

"Still, I would wish to go," muttered Young Gunty, his eyes shining. Carolanna looked at him fearfully.

"Pah!" his father grunted. "Wait until you have wisdom—and sons to care for the wife you leave behind."

"By then the white men's lodges will be sprouting in these woods like toadstools," grumbled Young Gunty. "And the trees will be felled for timber to build them."

"Not these two," Goody Cakebread pointed out, "for they were standing when these children came through, whenever that's to be. Dear me, it *is* confusing. But hadn't we best send them back through quickly? Unless I much mistake me, I hear horses on the road."

"Wim first," urged Rosemary, hoping to be last. Clutching Baba's hand, she watched Pala Ramanoke bring the sleepy little boy forward and set him on his feet.

"Time to go home, Wim." Baba pointed. "The nice man says home's that way."

Rosemary crossed her fingers.

Wim nodded. "G'home," he said. And he went.

"Lord preserve us, it's true!" gasped Goody Cakebread. In her fright she clutched Oliver Tolliver so tightly that he gave an indignant yowl and leaped straight into Baba's arms.

He leaped just as Baba stepped onto the shadowy path.

"Oliver!" shrieked the old lady. "Oh, dear Oliver Tolliver, come back . . ." Her call died away in the silent wood.

But suddenly the wood was no longer silent. A horse neighed, and there was the soft drum-and-rustle of hooves on the leafy track.

"Widow Cakebread?" It was a deep and cautious voice. "Be that you?"

The old lady gasped. "Do you know, I think that's my Tom. Could it be my Tom?"

"Quickly, before you're seen!" Gunty Ramanoke gave Rosemary a gentle push, but she twisted aside and caught at Goody Cakebread's hand.

"I don't *want* to go. I want to know what happens. I want to *know*." She was almost in tears.

"Goody Cakebread did not hear. "It *is* my Tom, my dear boy!" Pulling free, she pattered off down the track.

Old Gunty took Rosemary's hand. "Do not weep, owlet. Only think: if you stay, you will never learn what happens to those you care for in your own time. Yet if you go, you may ferret out the ending of our tale, for then it will have ended. Quickly now!"

Home for Dinner

The last thing Rosemary saw was Goody Cake-bread as she met the two riders who had pulled up in a pool of moonlight. A tall man in a dark cloak leaped down to the fold the old woman in a bearish hug as she squeaked, "My *dear* Tom!" The smaller of the two riders, a dark, fur-caped woman with sleepy eyes, and sparkly rings on her fingers, carried a wicker basket before her on the saddle. The half-grown cat sitting in the basket was a tortoise-shell tom.

"For you," said the dark woman to Goody Cake-bread. "Hees name ees Tophet."

And then she might have widened her sleepy dark eyes, for Rosemary winked out of sight.

For a moment Rosemary was out of her own sight too. She heard voices but saw nothing. A man's voice said, "You wouldn't reconsider about the house? I could go to seventy-five thousand for the house and the acreage down to the shore. Or did you buy that?" The voice was very like Tom Cakebread's, but it went on to say, "You only got the house by a fluke, you know. If I'd been getting my letters regularly, I'd have been home before Uncle George died, but I came down out of the El Tajín hills to find three months' worth of mail being held for me in Vera Cruz."

"I've landed in the wrong place," thought Rosemary wildly.

But then it was Aunt Sibby's voice, saying firmly, "How were your Uncle George's lawyers to know you weren't dead too? 'Historic Edifice' or no, they were happy to get the old place—and its leaky roof—off their hands. I was twice as pleased to have it. Still am."

Rosemary rubbed her eyes. Aunt Sibby and a strange man were sitting on a patchwork quilt in the center of a neatly mown lawn, surrounded by the remains of tea and sandwiches and cake. No Baba and no Wim.

Then it hit Rosemary. *Neatly mown lawn?* She looked around frantically. The ivy vines had been cut back and the clippings tidied away. The herb garden had been swept free of leaves and the earth spaded up. The smell of leaf-smoke drifted over the hedge from the direction of the front driveway, where a plume of white smoke rose.

The Time was gone.

"But it's my *home*," the man was saying persuasively. He was big and very nice-looking, Rosemary noticed vaguely. But who was he? His dark hair was peppered with gray, but there was a young and very mischievous glint to the smile he turned on Aunt Sibby. "I lived here with my grandmother until I was sixteen."

"*We* lived here every summer from the time I was four," countered Aunt Sibby, giving a little one-shoulder shrug. "And this old garden was the best of it all. Once I even . . . No, I won't sell it back. I—" She jumped as Parsley leaped into her lap. "Good heavens, Parsley! Mind the teacup. And Rosemary! Where did you pop out from?"

"This garden," said Rosemary wildly. "What's happened to it? Where's the stuff that grew here?" She stamped her foot on the stone.

"The herb garden? Why, Mr. Helps is going to plant us a new one. When he finished the roses, he offered to come tidy up in here so that we could use . . ." Suddenly she went very pale, and her teacup rattled so loudly in its saucer that the gentleman gave her a very curious look.

"Rosemary," Aunt Sibby croaked, clearing her

throat, "this is Mr. William Wingard, who's staying to dinner." She spoke very rapidly, as if she were afraid to stop. "Mr. Wingard teaches archaeology at the University of New Hampshire when he's not off digging up ancient cities. Mr. Wingard—er, Bill, this is my niece, Rosemary Walpole. Rosemary, I thought you must have walked down to the shore or the village. We looked everywhere for you an hour or so ago. You weren't in here all the time, were . . ." The words trailed off into a whisper.

"Baba!" said Rosemary. It came out in a scritchy little gasp. "You're Baba!"

Full Circle

Aunt Sibby's teacup landed upside down in the grass. "I thought it was a dream," she whispered. "I've been telling myself it was a dream ever since I was eight.

"I should have known. I should have known from the minute I saw you at the airport. I should have remembered." Aunt Sibby looked as if she couldn't decide between being appalled and being excited.

Mr. Wingard was forgotten. Rosemary kept saying, "Hepsibah Walpole!" Even after a cup of cold tea and half a smoked salmon sandwich, she could hardly believe it. "But you said *Sage*. You said your name was Hepsibah Sage."

Dazedly, Aunt Sibby said, "I suppose I wanted

it to be. With Mother and Father and Quincy all so unbearably—er, stuffy, I was sure I was adopted. I don't remember why the 'Sage.' Unless . . ." She grinned. "Unless it was from my middle name: Sagacity. Hepsibah Sagacity Walpole."

Rosemary giggled. "That's as bad as Daddy's."

"Quincy Rectitude Walpole? His suits him," said Aunt Sibby dryly, recovering. "I suppose Sage sounded both wiser and more pleasant. As in 'Parsley Sage.' " She tilted the old cat's chin up with one finger. "You looked wise even as a kitten, didn't you?"

Rosemary gave the cat a hard look. "Parsley *took* me," she said slowly. "Do you suppose he took me to help you get back?"

Mr. Wingard's head turned from Rosemary to Aunt Sibby and back like a spectator's at a tennis match.

"Perhaps," Aunt Sibby said. "I remember only bits and pieces. I remember Wim, and the piglet in the cupboard . . ."

"And going off to jail with the pigs and the cupboard?"

"Yes!" Aunt Sibby's eyes narrowed in concentration. "I was frightened, but you weren't. There was something about . . . yes, you were more upset about being late home for dinner. Heavens! That would have been *tonight*'s dinner." She shook her head in wonder. "How queer that we should have

gone back nearly twenty years apart and landed together. And I *am* glad that I didn't dream up—what was her name? Carolanna?—Carolanna and young Gunty. I used to make up stories about what had happened to them."

Rosemary sobered. "*I* wish we knew what happened to Goody Cakebread."

"And her cupboard." Aunt Sibby laughed.

"Er, um—this is all very fascinating," Mr. Wingard said, finally getting a word in. "But I don't understand what's happened. If you'll tell me what in blazes you're talking about, I might be able to tell you something about the Cakebreads."

"You? Why, yes, of course, if your family's lived here next to forever. It's this garden," Aunt Sibby began.

"Don't forget the sundial . . ."

"The wall must have opened up, and . . ."

"There was the plant in the herb garden, too. . . ."

"It's the craziest story I ever heard," said Bill Wingard, when it had all been straightened out. "For a moment there I almost . . . well, never mind that. The craziest part is that so much of it should be true. Come now, admit it: you two have been reading the old Cakebread diaries in the library."

"Diaries?"

"In the Bennickport Library?" Aunt Sibby was incredulous. "I thought all they had were the Bobbsey Twins and Zane Grey."

Mr. Wingard gave her a look of mock reproof. "No, in Uncle George's library. It was sold with the house, wasn't it? He inherited a lot of old histories and family papers from Grandma, and Grandma, before she married my grandfather, was a Cakebread."

Just What Happened

Before either Rosemary or Aunt Sibby recovered enough from their surprise to smother Mr. Wingard with questions, the clanging of a handbell from the direction of the house brought all three to their feet.

"Is it dinnertime already?" Aunt Sibby stamped her foot in frustration. "We'll have to go in. Mrs. Helps will be furious if we let her leg of lamb get cold. She's still fussing over how much we had to pay for it."

Bill Wingard grinned. "I shall tell my tale between courses." Waving Aunt Sibby through the arbor first, he caught up to walk beside her, one hand resting lightly on her shoulder. Rosemary frowned at that. Hadn't they just met? And he was *old*. Well, older than Aunt Sibby. Maybe thirty-five. *Forty*, even.

As dinner progressed from lobster soup to lamb and baby carrots to a splendid meringue cake topped with strawberries and whipped cream, Rosemary and Aunt Sibby heard the end of Goody Cakebread's adventures—in installments, for eager audience or no, Mr. Wingard took time to put away quite a bit of Mrs. Helps' good cooking.

Fifteen-year-old Thomas Cakebread ("That would be your Goody's Tom," said Bill) had run away to sea in 1710, and was not heard from again until the autumn of 1722. On an October night of that year, he drew up at the doorstep of the Mill House in Bennickport, mounted on a fine saddle horse, leading another, and followed by three carters driving three mountains of furniture and baggage, and a trim black man driving a trim black carriage, in which rode a green parrot, a parti-colored cat, and the beautiful Mrs. Thomas Cakebread.

For Tom had made his fortune. Three fortunes, to be precise: one in the rum and molasses trade between Barbados and the port of Boston, a second from his Barbados bride Juditha (whose papa owned five sugar plantations), and a third from Juditha's wise investment of their profits from the first two.

Two minutes after the angry Thomas had left the frightened miller quaking on his doorstep, the news was on its way around the village. Old Miller Cakebread's son had come back dressed like a lord and followed by a train of wagons. He had come not knowing his father was five years dead and had gone away in a rage at hearing that his old mother was shut up in York Gaol. Parson Grout had best look out!

Thomas wasted no time. He hammered on the marshall's door, and with that poor soul in tow, roused Town Clerk Wiggleton's household. Those two gentlemen, hatless, with greatcoats flung over their nightshirts, were hustled into the black carriage and whisked away to York, willy-nilly. It was not easy to refuse an angry young gentleman in a rich cloak trimmed with silk braid and collared with beaver—not when the fist he waved in your face glowed with a great ruby in a fat gold ring.

In York they found Goodwife Cakebread fled, and her gaolers dead to the world. The marshall and clerk were left to deal with Parson Grout, who, according to the eager-to-be-on-the-winning-side Wiggleton, had long shown a greedy interest in the Cakebread timberlands where the old lady had built her hovel. The marshall had agreed. "Set on having them, he was. Now I think on it, all that witchery talk came after y'r mother refused to sell." Together they tipped imaginary hats to young Mrs. Cakebread and her diamond rings and marched off to the Sample house to find the Grouts.

Back in Bennickport, Tom and Juditha left the carriage at the Compass Inn with the carts and carters, had fresh horses saddled up, and galloped out toward the elm woods. Whatever they found when they got there ("We needn't go into that.") apparently surprised and delighted Mistress Juditha.

For Juditha *was* a witch. The real thing. She admitted it in her diary, which was to have been burned and wasn't. Moreover, she was a shrewd, commonsensical practitioner of the art, not your everyday huggery-muggery Barbados witch. There were no secret words over secret fires, no waxen dollies stuck with pins. Juditha hadn't the slightest interest in frightening soft-witted souls or forcing them to do her will. Like the needle-witted grandmother from whom she learned her craft, Juditha's watchwords were *Employ Caution, Enjoy Comfort*, and *Indulge Curiosity*.

And the scene in the elm wood was marvelously curious to one who knew something of the ancient lore of trees.

"Yonder," said Juditha firmly, "we build our house. And here we build a wall to keep de trespassers from betwixt such . . . *interesting* trees."

So they did, and Goodwife Cakebread finished her life in great comfort. Parson Grout disappeared.

Thomas bought back the village mill and, adding a sawmill to it, kept the new miller on at Mill House as his agent. Thomas oversaw the work on the new house in the woods, with its roomy wing for his aged mother, and delighted that old lady with tales of his adventures. Juditha for her part laid out the gardens, ordered a bronze sundial cast in Rome, Italy, to her own peculiar design, and saw to the building of a handsome stone wall, doubled along the elm-tree side, to enclose the great trees completely. ("She even left them growing room so they wouldn't nudge the wall down.")

At the very last, when her marble stepping-stones had arrived from Boston, and Goodwife Cakebread's homely herbs had been transplanted into the little garden by the wall, Juditha made one final addition.

From a blackened wooden box addressed to *Mme Tomás Cakebird* from Vilcapampa, Peru, by way of Barbados, she unwrapped a small clump of green from a cocoon of moss and sacking and planted it beneath the gleaming sundial. Her diary said, *This day the T. planted, having arriv'd much crimped from the smallness of the box. Now the Way is open only to those with the Key, which is to say, My Self.*

Bill Wingard shut the small leatherbound volume. "The rest you can probably guess. The secret was passed from Juditha to her daughter-in-law, and in turn to *her* son's wife. By the time it came down to my grandmother, nothing was left of it but a bone or two—a story to tell children on a winter evening."

"And we stumbled onto the combination," said Aunt Sibby thoughtfully. "Three o'clock—on Midsummer Eve—on just that spot."

"Standing in the center of Time," finished Rosemary triumphantly. Her face fell as she remembered the uprooted Time.

"So you say." Bill slipped the diary back among the other books on the topmost shelf. "I see you've kept old *Early Days* and all the rest," he drawled.

"Oh, but I couldn't keep them now. They're yours. Your family records." Aunt Sibby was insistent.

"You'll just keep the house, is that it?" Bill laughed and pulled down *Bennickport: the Early Days*. "Here, this is what the two of you have been reading." He riffled through the pages and stopped at an engraving with the caption *The Miller and his Wife*. The woman was Goody Cakebread to the life.

"Oh, dear," said Aunt Sibby.

There were several others: *The Saco Sachem, Gonotee Rumnoak and his Wife*, one of Town Clerk Wiggleton, and *Prospect of the County Gaol in York*.

"What do you say to that?"

"But," said Rosemary desperately, "I scarcely looked at the pictures, and I never read who they were. Honestly."

"And *I* never opened that book until . . ." Aunt Sibby's protest died as a too-casual movement caught her eye. "Aha! Now what would you be slipping into your pocket so sneakily?"

Bill shrugged and said offhandedly, "Nothing. Just an old photograph of me Grandma must have tucked into Juditha's diary. A silly baby picture."

Aunt Sibby's green eyes narrowed suspiciously. "Oh? May I see it?"

Bill's hand closed around her outstretched one. "Oh, no you don't. Not until you know me better." Holding on, he grinned maddeningly. "You will, you know."

He was too busy enjoying Aunt Sibby giving off sparks to see the small hand that twitched the photo from his pocket. Only when Sibby's sparks became a twinkle did his hand fly to his pocket.

"All right, Rosie. Hand it over."

But a wide-eyed Rosemary was already looking at the back side of the old snapshot of a toddler in diapers wearing a wide ribbon that said *1939* across his chest. As she read, her eyes grew rounder still.

"Rosemary? Let me see." Aunt Sibby darted around Bill's reach and snatched the photo.

The inscription on the back read:

Wim
(William Jr.)
at the Parkers' New Yrs Party.
Aged 18 months.

And Tomorrow

Standing on the front doorstep at ten o'clock, Bill —or Wim—was still insisting, "I don't remember a thing."

"But you *do* believe us about the adventure." Aunt Sibby peered at him in the dim porch light. "I know you believe us. Even Parsley knows you believe us. See? You're the first man he's ever taken to. He *knows* you know."

Bill raised an eyebrow at the old cat leaning against his ankle. "Do you indeed? I wonder. Interesting, though: he looks like the old tom grandma had. Must be his grandson."

"*I* think he's the same cat. From even before Oliver Tolliver," said Rosemary stoutly.

Aunt Sibby's laugh rang out like a bell. "Rosemary, your parents aren't going to know you come August. There won't be a solid four-cornered fact left in your head. They'll ship you right back by the next flight."

Then she sighed. "And *we* haven't a fact between us to convince this Mr. Wingard-Cakebread . . . *oops!*"

Rosemary was as astonished as Aunt Sibby. One minute Bill Wingard was turning toward his car and the next he was on the top step, kissing Sibby a very firm good-night.

"Just presuming on an old acquaintance," he said blandly. "All very proper if we've known each other since 1722, as you insist. Good night, my dear. Good night, Rosemary. Be ready at nine o'clock in the morning. I'll pick up the two of you then."

"What . . . what for?" managed Aunt Sibby, weakly.

"That cupboard." Bill crunched across the driveway to his car. "Juditha's diary never once mentions it, and it's in none of the old Wychwood inventories. We'll start down at York Gaol. See if they have any record of it."

Aunt Sibby, having caught her breath, gathered her wits. "What cupboard?" she asked innocently. "If the diaries don't mention it, you have only our word that it existed, and we know what you think of our word."

"Oh, your word is good. Didn't I tell you?" he said even more innocently. "It's true that I don't remember a scrap of the adventure, but my grand-mother did tell me about the time I got lost. It seems she found me in the herb garden hours later, dressed in a peculiar smock and brown woolen leggings and buckled shoes. She kept them. They're probably in your attic."

The car door slammed. "Nine o'clock," he called, and was gone in a spray of gravel.

"Do you know, we *didn't* change him back," exclaimed Rosemary. "His clothes, I mean."

"What?" Aunt Sibby was staring up the drive. "Oh, yes; good night, dear."

At the top of the stairs Rosemary sat down to think. It was all very clear which way the wind was blowing. Bill was going to get his house back. And Aunt Sibby . . .

Rosemary thought glumly of home, where noth-ing was ever a puzzle or an adventure. "I wonder," she said to Parsley Sage, who had followed her up, "*would* Mother and Daddy ship me right back?"

Parsley landed in her lap in a kittenish leap and stretched up to sandpaper her chin with his tongue. Rosemary looked at him thoughtfully.

She would plan carefully just what to say. . . .